EDEN *miniatures*

THE PLANET WALK

© 2018 by FREI

The Planet Walk

First Edition

The Planet Walk was first published as part of *EDEN by FREI – a concept narrative in the here & now about the where, the wherefore and forever* at *EDENbyFREI.net*

All rights reserved. No part of this publication may be reproduced, stored in a retrieval system or transmitted in any form or by any means, electronic, mechanical, photocopying, recording or otherwise without the prior permission of the publisher or in accordance with the provisions of the Copyright, Designs and Patents Act 1988.

The right by FREI to be identified as the author of this work has been asserted by them in accordance with the Copyright, Designs and Patents Act 1988.

ISBN: 978-1-64255-369-7

Optimist Books by Optimist Creations

The Planet Walk

Preamble

I whirl within the wherefores of my wonder

still coming at me are the satellites, the
comets, the debris —

celestial collisions

I am at home here, though my longing knows
no boundaries now, no aim

knows no deliverance from thought, from
search for meaning

would my soul took over

would my skin shirked not the touch, would
I felt this fear of losing were not real, this
holding on, this

need for explanations, this

THE PLANET WALK

reluctance

*ever to surrender to what is: what is this if
not ice not gas not water and not energy,
what is*

the reason

*reason holds me, holds me in or back; then
back from what, back where, back to what
end?*

is there an end?

There's no beginning, then how is there

reason?

Neptune

I sit on the edge of the solar system, with Neptune, invisible. I'm known to exist, but nobody sees me. I think I see them, from a distance, through a haze. I can't be sure. Twinkles, here and there, allover really: wondrous...

I have, inadvertently, become a god. This is both puzzling and absurd: those powers they invest in me are merely mythical. I am not even drawn to water, not as other people are. Some see the sea and jump right in. I don't. I am content to sit there, pondering. Until the time comes. Until I'm ready. Until I feel the need. Until curiosity gets the better of me. Or temptation. Or just the wanting to have been in the water

not been in the water at all. For a moment.
Or two. With the lover, the dolphins, the
mermaids, the waves and the fishes. The
other gods. This propensity to ponder. It
may be an affliction; but why not. 'Why
not?' seems to be the overriding question.
Is that what it is: a question?

I walk from Neptune towards the sun
through the snow – like shooting stars,
falling. I love the snow falling on my face
as I look up at the sky, at the space, at these
planets, the aboveness and the aroundness
of it all; the path ahead is white and clear,
and there's no-one about. Of course
not: I'm alone. Alone on the edge of the
universe.

A pang of love, a moment of pain. Love for
whom? Pain of what? A special one now,
this time, really? A sense of myself, now,

really? Or of the idea of myself. Of the Concept. The Unreality.

I like my reality right now, I can deal with it, I can live up to it, make sense of it, or so I tell myself, knowing this not to be true, not entirely.

I walk, steadily—not fast, not slow—along the path of the planets, thinking myself Neptune. I am not a planet. I am not a god. I am not a myth. I feel millions of miles away from the allness of it all, but I'm about to dissolve into it, and this thrills me.

Is that a lonely path I walk or is it just deserted? Because it's late. Because it's out of season. Because it normally is, around now. Is it *too late?* This turns into a portentous question all of a sudden. Am I too far along the path, do I circle too planets, we are not rivers, we are barely human.

We are human. So bare though, so vulnerable, so thoughtful, so cautious, so hesitant, so almost capable. So willing, yet, to survive. So surviving. Thriving, even, against the odds. So gentle. So soft. So curly, the hair. So even the teeth. So tender the lips. So lovely the legs. So quirkily satin the belly button. So elegant the fingers. So delicate the eyelashes. So warm, so warm though the chest.

So fleeting, so insubstantial as I walk under fir trees and the snow they are clothed in, so naked, so wrapped up in my delusion, my reading the signs that aren't there, my wanting it all to be and to mean something. Wanting it all. To be and to mean. Something.

I take pictures of the snow so I can send them to him, though I don't even know if he wants to look at the snow through my lens through my eyes through the synapses of my brain that miss him, but I know he has never seen snow for real and I want to show it to him. His mind is not here any more than his body. What of his soul? It sits right in me. He would love the snow, I know, if he saw it for real. If he were with me now. If we were insubstantial now in the snow together, seeping into the ground.

I know these things. I now know them all, and they all make sense, and they will come to pass, and it all just needs time to arrange itself now. I want to be sure.

I missed Uranus on my journey, I realise, as I pass Saturn, wondering why that took so long, and I don't mind. There's an even a pun. Not a sign. It's a coincidence: sometimes you miss a planet, that's all.

I'd decided to surrender, to go with the flow, just to be. I'm calm at the thought, now, at ease. I feel a greater certainty than ever before, but I'm not sure about what. Just about. And I know I don't need to investigate this, I don't need to probe.

I don't need to understand, because I already know. I don't want to be the one any more who longs. I don't want to be the one any more who pines and freezes. The one made of ice. And rocks. Enveloped in abundant gases. Who errs on the side of reason, out of sight, out of mind, out of being. I want to thaw and to melt and to meld with the one and to bloom and to lose myself in the all and to be.

Jupiter

I shall return to Saturn. I'll not ignore it,
not have passed it for good, unawed by
its majesty, unwondered by its spheres.
Unswayed. It sways me, Saturn; but
not now. Now I am drawn on further,
down—not down, across—the path: the
gravitation is too strong, its presence too
immense, I must succumb to Jupiter. For a
moment. For a while.

For an eternity that lasts a fraction of a
thought. For a whirl of a gas storm. For a
communion. With Callisto. Io, Ganymede.
Europa. These friends I have not met.
These habitations. These absorptions;
moments, these ideas. Sensations. My body,
more than my spirit, attracts them and
they me. We enter each other's orbits, and

THE PLANET WALK

to a planet all of their own, but I enjoy
them, their company, their zest, their life.
Their juvenation. I visit them, they me. We
journey not together, we relish the here.
The nowness of it all, it is not mere. Have I
not longed so long to be in the now?

This here is good, I like it, though it will
not, doesn't have to, last. The mightiness
that overshadows us encumbers us not: we
are not oblivious, but we don't care; choose
not to be intimidated by this massiveness,
this bold inelegance.

The world right now, that world that
is not this world and that is this world
still though we may never wish it so, it
bears great force, great danger; anger too.
But not for us. We delicate ourselves out
of its artless rage. We are not like that. Are
not of it. It not of us. I no longer feel the

need to explain myself, and I no longer long for the need to be free.

I am free, now, having got this far, and I relish that freedom more than I treasure my life. I am not Jupiter, nor ever want to be. That bulk, that pompousness. That body of hot air, covered in cold. That implacability. That dehumanising fervour.

And yet, these satellites, seductive with their charm. I'm glad I came here. Happy to have paused. I've long abandoned the idea of destination. These are sojourns on a celestial perambulation. How privileged I am. How powerful. How small.

Here, seeing Jupiter be big, be brash, though not beguiling, I believe my time has come. This is not new, I'd thought on one or two occasions once or twice before

THE PLANET WALK

I realise my strength is not outwith. You
may be one and a half score septillion
times the size of me, but you are no match
to my mind. You have the mass; the sun
has all the power: I have the intellect. To
survive, to thrive even. To discern. To
accommodate myself in this universe, or
any other.

I launder my library of references by
adding experience. The hunger to live.
The need to swallow. The acceptance
of millions of potentialities in one go.
The taste and the texture. A slither of
hope, of forbearing, of premonition. A
spark of the imagination; a tenderness,
returned. And wanted. Handsomenesses.
No warriors, these, no battle axe ire, no
strategy and no plan. No tactics. No
goal. A glorious swim in the sea, a pool
of tadpoles of random configurations, a

Ye godlinesses. Ye buds of brimming boisterousness. Ye flowers and sparks. Ye spermly waggers of tails. Ye lusciousnesses. Ye beetrootjuiceredvoluptuousness. Ye inspiration.

Ye words.

Saturn calls me back, I know. I'll have to detour there, a loop. This Jupiter wilfulness cannot last. I feel for Ganymede, I feel for Europa. Ye Kepler-452b. I feel for you too. I feel for my brother who is writing these words in a universe just like ours only different, having acceded that that's what he's doing without knowing why. I feel for my coccyx; I feel for you.

I feel for you and I sense you are there, and I feel strongly for a new love a new warmth a new glow a new smile a new touch of

a new tuft of hair *and* a belly button; a
new mind, a new generous heart on the
horizon. Where is the horizon, in space,
in the orbit of Jupiter, near one of his
moons? I baffle myself into submission and
accept the reality as it is, though I know
full well that there is no such thing; and
there is no such thing as necessity, distance,
perspective or pain. There is pain, it is felt,
it is lived. Does it have to be, ever? It need
not be celebrated quite so. There is no hate,
it is an illusion, and there is no anger, it
disappears. There is there is there is love.

I like that thought and take comfort in
it although I can't prove it, and I think
of my new love on the horizon whom
I haven't yet met. Literally, have not
yet met. We know each other, we are in
communication, we are getting closer all
the time, but the whisper of the unknown

longer, not because we want to, but because we want to believe that we must. So we must. So we do. We're pragmatic like that, and we have lives to live. So we think, so we hope, so we trust.

I salute Jupiter for all his preposterousness and kiss each of his moons goodbye. I'm not sure I need to come back here: this was great, this was fun, this was excellent, while it lasted. But possibly, probably, for me, it has now run its course.

I bid thee farewell, most mighty of planets: you have been, I know, quite misunderstood. But don't worry, my gaseous friend, so have we all...

Mercury

My mentality makes me leap as close to the
sun as I may without being burnt, without
floating adrift, without losing my sense of
belonging, if not here, if not there, then in
the universalness of it all.

There is something wondrous about being
me, still, at this age, at this point, which is
never a point only but always a wave just
as much; at this juncture which is never a
coming together only, but always as much
a moving apart, through this phase which
is never as much a beginning as it is also an
ending, only more so, which means it just
is; there is intemperance, folly, wisdom and
wit to be found where there's light, and
there's the mischief of knowledge: am I

THE PLANET WALK

Here on Mercury where a day lasts a
couple of years at least by perception,
my mind is blasted by solar winds, and I
take hold of my wand, meaning to keep
it. The power to lull the awake into sleep,
to awaken those lost to slumber, to ease
the agony of the dying and to quicken the
dead. The quickness, the quirkinesses, the
quintessentialness of it all.

I race around the sun looking out into
space, and I enjoy the ride more than ever
I did before. How come youth arrives at
an age when it is all but gone? How come
it happens twice? The first time with no
experience on the fabric of sensations
to handle it well, the second time with
said fabric so worn that it feels all but
threadbare? Will there be a third instance,
maybe a fourth? Is it necessary, possible,
even, to count?

My brain cells refuse to collapse, and my
curiosity gets the better of me, so I keep
carving open new synapses, firing new
thoughts into a continuum that is already
awash with ideas.

No time, no space, no respite, no rest,
no melancholy here, no decay: this iron
is liquid is hot is alive with pure energy,
not organic, not systemic, not caustic,
not quiet, not loud: effervescent in its
potential. This place may be small, but its
capacity to astonish is great, nay unlimited,
nay infinite and profound.

Can lovers be friends? Can pleasures
bedevil the heart that has grown to
be kind? Can connections be the
meaningfulness of it all? The essentiality?
The reason? The cause? The spark and the
fire, but also the balm? Can this toxicity

of spirit ask more than questions? What is
there beyond the surprise, the delirium at
having recognised I am able to speak? Am
I the medium or the message or merely the
conduit? Would I mind if I knew, could I
know if I cared?

There are now too many possibilities,
too many strands, too many fluctuations,
and too many rotations; too many rules
that like laugh lines adorn me for me to
worry: care I may, yes, and consider; learn
I can, and communicate, lend a gentle
ear, sometimes, and a generous eye, and
embrace the love that is not mere emotion,
but more than instinct is intellect, and
say yes: I comprehend. Not understand,
perhaps, not everything, yet, quite possibly
not ever—things move so fast, so all over—
but I can take it all in. I can be it all. I can
be little and insignificant and still mean

to sense. There is no mirror here on this
planet, Narcissus has settled on Earth, and
my ego today is not needy, nor never will
be, no more: my eccentricity here is at its
most extreme, at its most exquisite, most
extraordinarily acute, and I'm comfortable
with that too.

I call on my younger self to excuse my
inadequacies, as I know my older self
will be looking across to me now as I
am and merely encourage, not chide,
because I have here now forgiven my older
self its obliviousness, its perfection. Its
contradiction, in terms. This, for all its
unreasonable demeanour, is maybe the
best position I've been in. And I've been
everywhere, but not yet. Soon this, too,
must come to a premature end if it is to last
forever, and that's what it is.

Venus

Venus troubles me. I come here reluctantly;
so bright. So mystifying, so inscrutable. So
tenebrous, as well, beneath that gleaming
skin. Moist. Overwhelming, warm; so
uninhabitable, at least for me.

And still I feel I ought to spend some
time here. Wherefore, I know not. For
the experience? For the completion of
my being? For the expansion, yet, of my
horizon? These planets travel far and yet
not wide, except they do. They are—we all
are—on a forward motion we don't notice.

Venus knows. This is a body that's imbued
with universal wisdom, which it can't
express. We move in spirals, not ellipses,

but we're a little further down our path: it's
not the direction of our nose that we travel
in, it is the direction of our pate. We have
no eyes there, at the top of our head, we
have only a string that pulls us, and still we
resist.

Here on Venus, everything feels strange;
the smells, the flavours, the embrace. The
fuzzinesses and the softness, they unsettle
me. Long before I become comfortable
I become complacent, and that will not
do. I start to fidget, restless. I think I am
getting ready to settle in some sort of
way, but settledness entails a great deal of
immobility. I like the rest of motion. I need
to be alone. Not all the time, but enough.
Venus asks me too many questions. It's
not that I can't find any answers, these
answers can mostly be found, but the
effort is out of proportion. The thinking

here. The obviousnesses, the courtship; the irrationalities, repetitions.

At the time there was no myth and no meaning. The time being the beginning, the beginning being the origin, the origin being unknown. I suddenly feel alert, a little, and happier to exist, mainly because of this old realisation that I can't, I just can't expect myself to make sense of it all. Any of it, really, it's just there. Annoying as it may be. I take a step back, and I look at my thoughts as they spread out before me, and find them unsatisfactory. The thinking I'm doing is inelegant, crude; it will not suffice. Nor is it poetic. And thinking without poetry is like love without mathematics. It has no substance, no structure, no special tingle of satisfaction, no meaning. It is like sex in a haze of drunkenness with someone you don't fancy. I'm becoming self-referential and it irks me.

Womanhood. Much like aliens, women don't so much scare me as baffle. I've hardly ever thought this through, but there comes a time. And a place. I seriously doubt that now is that time or this that place, but when or where will it ever be, and does it matter? I contend myself mostly with knowing that there are things I can't know, and go where my curiosity takes me, which is not normally here. Nor abnormally. I'm out of my depth, out of my comfort, out of my pond. The mountains, the seas and the rivers, the streams. The landscape and the disorientation. There are too many things happening all at once to get a handle on any of them, and there is also the new mix the new blend the new fusion. That both excites and frightens me, a little.

but because I really like my delineations
as much as I like my inbetweennesses and
my blurrage; the overlappedisation of our
existence, I like it. Entropy.

I hear a warm soothing voice that is not
in my head and it is not in my memory; it
is not my mother, my sister, my wife. The
voice comes from the ground and from
the cloud that envelops the ground and
from the all about the sphere that I have
wrapped my body around, and it says that
there are no mysteries and there must be
no sorrow. She's trying to reassure me, I'm
not sure she succeeds, but her sentiment
is kind. I feel her hand on my back on my
neck on my thigh, and the touch is tender
and real. I recall once upon a time being
deeply at ease in this presence and as deeply
afraid of it too. What embraces you may
ensnare you, what holds you can crush you,

own you. What owns you is you. And you thought you knew who you were.

Did I? Maybe a couple of aeons ago; it is possible, then, when I did not yet exist, that I was really quite sure of myself. I had an arrogant streak, not mean, not cocky, but aloof. My journey humbles me. I sense I'm getting closer to the truth, and like everyone else I know that there is no such thing, though deep down I want there to be, and maybe there is. If not a truth, then a value, perhaps, to hold on to.

The energy that we are. The quantum states. The potentialities. The particles and the waves. Of course I am Venus as much as Venus is me: we share the constituent parts, and yet: I don't belong here. It's sometimes good to know where you belong, and also good to know where you don't. There's

and does change, and you never say never
and all that goes with it, and in any case
there is only so much existing you can
expect to be doing at any one time, but by
the time your energy dissolves and changes
its form, time ceases too, and you are quite
literally reborn, only not in the way that
you thought you didn't want to think
about, or were taught, or wanted to believe
to be nonsense. From one state to another.
These states are all within us contained.
The energy that you are is your matter
your body your molecules your thoughts
your emotion your wants and your needs
(always, they come as a pair: you knew that
already), your shades and your textures,
and when they go they don't go, they
are simply reconfigured, because energy
cannot be destroyed, it can only, and will,
be transformed.

THE PLANET WALK

I shall not miss myself when I'm gone, for I
am always around. So are you, so is Venus.
So are the superclusters of our sistergods.

I am much happier now than I was before
I came here. I knew I would be, I doubted
it not. But now, much as I sense the draw
of the earth that is so near and so familiar
and so welcoming too, I must surely go on
a detour and find me a distant adventure.
Home beckons, but I have to explore…

Uranus

I wander to the place I know least and for a
while I maybe like best, in a way; as an idea,
as a thought, as a concept: the abstract
liking of something from which you are
distant, the fascination with unfamiliarity,
the lure of the other; the stranger, the
comfort, the awe.

The steady roll on an invisible plane, the
cool electric hue. The very slow seasons.
Even the unwitting humour, lame
though it is. It is a laconic planet I find
here, unruffled, smooth and cyan. The
awayness of it all, as at the end of despair.
A well-neighboured distance; bookended,
escorted by giants: significant in its own
right but overlooked, overshadowed and,

THE PLANET WALK

There is no life here, but there is otherness, and that in itself is interesting. It feeds my curiosity: to go a step further, to move beyond. To tumble on a different axis, to fall upwards; float frozen but not still, to sense a different kind of heat on a newly defined horizon. I expect to be alone here, but I'm surrounded by character: here, in the outskirts, in the slow moving cold, there are others like me: how did we all get here? What projected us into this orbit, so far away, it would seem, from the soul, so within?

These layers, these clouds, these rocks and these crystals, these rings, this ice and these moons, this magnetotail. They are not, perhaps, home, but they are a meaning all in themselves, and they are somewhere, beautiful. True.

For quite some time I enjoy this
tangentiality and become part of it,
willingly, coolly; I relish the arm's length
attention I get. Nobody knows me here,
or cares who I am, but my aloofness my
look and my languid demeanour are being
noted. My hair the peroxide silver of this
unbreathable atmosphere and my clothes
the black of the all that surrounds me. If
you know where I am you can find me, and
find me foreign and alien too.

Yet after a while I miss the simplicity
of warmth. Not that I know what that
means, but it means that I'm out in the
cold, and I want to come back now,
closer to home, closer to the sun, closer to
people who don't understand me, closer
to something I vaguely remember as love.
This strangeness leaves me estranged from
myself, and enjoying it now seems an effort.

realise now that I'm not living my life in chronological order. That puzzles me for a moment until it occurs to me that time too is down to perception, and there will come a time when it'll all simply blend into one, as it must.

Entropy.

(Yet still, yet again, only more so, always more...)

Out here I thought I felt a sense of freedom, until that sense became quite oppressive. That, too, was a surprise. And so I let go. Slowly, at first and then readier, more. This is not for me, after all, this agreeable spectacle, this isolation: it could quite easily turn into a habit, a mannerism, a cliche, a role.

The young man at a *soirée* (it was that more
than it was a party, a dinner, or drinks)
who'd looked at me and said: 'are you for
real?' That's when I knew I was in danger
of becoming a caricature of myself, and
Uranus could be my place no more.

I like this now, this clarity, this resolution.
This immense relief too, not to have to be
defined by weirdness forever. Strange, yes,
curious, always, different, maybe (then
'different' to what?), but not impenetrable
and not obscure.

Not even, in that sense, mysterious, really:
there are so very few mysteries in the
universe, apart from the multiverse of all
possible universes itself, and that, too, is
only a matter of consciousness and the
cumulative number of brain cells firing at
it: one day it will be just another reality

too. Like blossoms, like spring. Like the awakening, too.

I'm getting better at this, being me. This walk seems to be doing wonders...

Saturn

Dione, Tethys, Mimas, Enceladus –
your friendly moons' names sound like
characters to me, in a pastoral play.
Even Titan and Iapetus; they have been
overthrown, dwell in the pantheon no
longer: neighbours now, living downstairs,
or, to wave at, across the street.

Your rings, though no more mysterious
now than you, are delicate still; and you are
inviting too. Against thy will, methinks;
like the old rustic who grumbles at first
and enjoys the thought of himself as
forbidding, but turns out to be at heart
quite congenial.

I am at the stage now where I feel there

fewer instances of despair. That can only,
I sense, be a good thing. Journeying has
put me at ease with myself. I feel millions
of miles away still from where I envisage
I should be, but this seems natural now,
and of little concern. The hereness and
thereness of it all: the potencies of the
potential. The meta nomenclature of the id.
The closer I get to being myself, the more I
disperse myself across the quanta of energy:
thought. Insubstantive meanderings that
then turn out to make sense after all. At
some point, at some level, in some way. Not
conscious, perhaps, but innocuous, calm.

I sit down on one of these rings and let
my legs dangle in the brook of what looks
from afar like a void that surrounds it, and
my toes tingle at the excitement of being
and wriggle with a childlike and clean and
unjaded joy: they haven't walked as far yet

Over the meadows of this spacescape, this
English garden, this *Ermitage*. I feel my
thin body, pale and slender but resilient
and robust, as it was back then, when I was
a boy. It never preoccupied itself with itself.
The etherealness of it all, the curiousness.
And always, always the wonder. Nobody
joins me, yet, and maybe none ever will
now, and it saddens me not, I am free.

From where I perch on my borrowed bank,
my legs suspended, my hand—the left
one—playing with marbles, the molecules,
the droplets, the pebbles and the whists of
yellow-blue algae that get trapped in my
fingers, cool and gentle, soft and strong,
my eyes, inclined toward what lies below
and therefore what also above, my face
reflected (reminiscent, perhaps, after all,
of Narcissus, though he, I know, does not
belong here any more than he does on

for a fleeting moment I wish me a one
for them to be kissed. The longing, the
curiosity, still, and the awe.

I am on the brink, I realise, and at this
point, sooner or later, there does come the
point where you have to decide. Do you
jump, assuming that you will fly, or don't
you, fearing that you might drown.

Why do I do this from here, and not
where I started? Have I conspired with
circumstances to manoeuvre myself onto
the fence of a planet whose patron is the
god of the farmer of all things to finally
return to the George in me and embrace
him as much as release him in exactly the
same gesture, at exactly the same time, for
exactly the same reasons and to exactly
the same end? It wouldn't surprise me.
Hardly anything would. The universe finds

whatever happens next is bound to happen,
just as what happened before was in its own
liquid way quite inevitable.

All the querulousnesses of adversaries
(they were friends in disguise), all the
insurmountablenesses of obstacles, varied
and frequent and each in its own right
unreasonable, from here, from this tholin
perspective, rotating at speed, and wobbly,
a little bit drunk on the juices of life, but
steady and safe in myself now—as far as
there even exist such notions as 'steadiness,'
'safety' and 'self'—look irrelevant now and
benign.

My right hand that has been holding on to
the ice, to the carbon, the substance, such
as there was, in a vain grip on something
the brain interpreted as 'reality,' still,
after only another decade or so of faint

THE PLANET WALK

I sink not, and nor do I soar: I float, once
again, now earthwards, I'm sure.

Mars

I knew this would happen. I knew I could
stay this, but not forever, I knew I would
have to confront it, I knew I would not get
away with keeping away: I'm on my way
home. The fact that I entertain a notion of
'home' is in itself a symptom of growing
up, surely. Growing in. Growing through.
Through the crises, the awaynesses of it all,
the doubts and the fear.

Between Horror and Terror I stand on the
Seat of the Gods and I feel me a warrior.
Hah! Who would have thought that
I could answer the call. Hold my head
high and keep my gaze straight and look
upon Earth in the distance and say: I
salute thee, Mother, and I charge thee to

hesitation, no confusion, and no offence.
This rust coloured dust, this thin-skinned
robustness. This unflappable sense of the
just. Of the righteous. Of the direct, of the
cause and the anger. The Anger. The wrath.

The *outrageousness* of it all. There's nothing
twee about it, nothing humorous, fun,
camp, harmless or charming. Ere I lose my
sense of proportion I shall steel my spine
to this ire. Stupidity, wantonness, cruelty
and fear. The stubborn ignorance of greed.
The tyrants, the egomaniacal butchers and
keepers of slaves. They are an *outrage*. One
as destructive, as unenlightened and as
inhumane as the other. There the slaughter
of innocents, the imposition of rule; the
indoctrination, the violence, the cult.
Here the wilful deception, the making
of unholy myths, the falsing of facts, the
aggrandisations and the buffoonness: the

rhetoric, the gestures, the meaningless
phrases, the orange, the hair.

The beateous soul in my sinuous body
wishes it were not so, but "nature is war,"
and until I dissolve into the particle waves
and the unnamed insubstantiality of
connexion, I have to make a stand and be
counted. Too long, maybe, have I tried to
avoid this. Too long shied away. Too long
have I hovered above ground thinking it
all—the dirt, the blood, the grit (that word
I never, ever, liked or was even willing to
use), the bone and the marrow, the shit, the
severed limbs, the crushed skulls and the
unwanted guts spilling into the mud, the
jealous, the mean, the preoccupied with
survival—thinking them and it all quite
beneath me. It is, of course, quite beneath
me, under my feet: will I or no, I trample
the trodden no less than the soldiers

to behave. Politeness. There is virtue in
civil conduct and in a refusal to simply
surrender, but form on its own now won't
function. Sad, sincerely, but so.

The scorn. To be put in this position.
To not be released. To have to respond.
To be set against something so real. So
unavoidably ugly. In this land of the alien.
On this inhospitable neighbour.

My sense of humanity and what I want it
to mean here is challenged, de-ranged. I
am out of joint, but not out of scope. These
forces can not be contained, perhaps, but
they can be conquered. With spirit, with
wisdom, with core. With arguments? No.
With reason? Not likely. With strength
(not with force) and with purpose. But it is
still a war. There are battles that need to be
won.

I survey the Plane of Utopia and pronounce this my moment of muster. Here of all places. This desert has nothing that I want to own except my presence, and that is now no longer negotiable. There comes the instance when you know that all else is mist. The haze doesn't clear yet, in the distance, but I do sense the bridge. This tying together of thoughts with the elements that are also in me, lest I ignore them. The substance that I fashion to my own design. Titanium and graphene. If there be materiality, make it exquisite, sophisticated and strong.

There is no feebleness in wanting good.

There is no harm in seeking softness. No despair in keeping faith.

There is no shame in hope, no loss of self in

THE PLANET WALK

Embracing all of it, being it and sending the
signal. I take me a cue from the lingering
trojans and inwardly smile, even laugh.
Haha! Now is the time to go forth.

I have no fear and no loathing and nothing
to prove. Less, still, have I to lose. I have
quite left me behind my despair. I see me
one coming towards me whom I may yet
be willing to join, or he me, and if that be
so then so much the better, there is a lion
yet to the eagle, but it is not the content,
and not the end, it is but a chance to make
some things completer, and I'm sure now
of the simplest of things: that I am.

Earth

And so, back. Down. To Earth. Where
I belong? *This,* my home? This desert
wilderness of beauty and voluptuousness,
this abundance of colour, vegetation,
insects and beasts; these cities, these people,
these civilisations? This art, these quantities
of stuff and rubbish; these tears, these
cruelties, these abominations? This joy?
These excellences, these wonders? These
tastes, these smells, these flavours, these
sensualities, these sweet transgressions,
these experiences? This catharsis? This
messiness, these quarrelsome foibles; these
imperfections, these obstacles? And this
weather?

This air that I breathe, this need to do

the road, these symbols, these signs? These
abstractions? These metaphors, this poetry,
this song and this dance? That we make?
About *what?* This love.

Everything suddenly feels disconcertingly
real again, and I'm not sure I like it. I'm
sure I don't dislike it, not as such, but I
find these certainties confusing. These
obligations to respond. These figures
of speech, these formulations. These
competitions for superlatives. These
hyperboles. These headlines, these star-
ratings, these ceremonies, these awards.
These absurdities. These traumas of
rejection or attraction, of interpretation
of behaviour of looks and of glances, these
whispered words, these games I refuse
to play. These rules. These obediences,
these categories, these schedules, these
expectations. These parochial wordlinesses.

This world perplexes, awes and bewilders me. Here I am, stunned to find myself on it, in it, part of it, and I am momentarily paralysed. This will not last, I feel sure, though why I should feel so I don't know.

For a long time now I have felt like wading through treacle, slowly, cumbersomely, glued to the ground by a sticky morass that would not let go. There is no escape from gravity in this place, except perhaps on aerial silks or on skis. The former are not for me, the latter very much so. I think me on the mountain, gliding down the glorious white, with the Alps in the distance and the molecules in my lungs, and I know what it is to be free. That I know; that, I can relate to. Everything else does not quite make sense. Which is strange: I've been learning and trying to me as the planets from which I've returned, richer in mind yet not much the wiser. At the end of the day there is always the here and now to make something of, and now that I'm here, I might as well make the most of it. Thus I tell myself, over again.

'Most' meaning 'best': meaning all I can do. What could that possibly be? If I allow my youth up to say about eighteen, nineteen – why not twenty-one: if I allow that to be my formative phase that doesn't yet count as my adult existence, then I'm now halfway at least through what my adult existence can reasonably be expected to be: I can still look forward, but as much can I, must I, look back. That frightens the hell out of me. That I'm here on Earth, effectively halfway through—way over, if you're counting from birth—feeling pretty much as I felt right at the beginning, and having really moved from the spot. Not having done more than tried, but without ever really succeeding, to take flight. Does that mean it's *too late?* Is it ever, can it ever be simply *too late?* But for what? For some sort of attainment, of *what?* Of acclaim, recognition, notoriety, 'fame'? Or even just *love?* Can love be *attained?*

"Be not afraid of moving slowly, be only afraid of standing still." I want to know what the soul is. At a quantum level: the science, the understandable, perceptible, conceptualisable part of existence that is not material, not intelligent, not rational, not emotional; intangible, insubstantial but essential and real. A Quantum Philosophy. I want to know what that is.

That part of me that I can't see when I look in the mirror and that I can't choose one of

express in words—and if I write another
million or ten—that I sense is forming and
taking shape (without shape, of course),
that is there and that others, some others,
recognise in an instant (others, of course,
never will): that is what interests me, makes
me curious to go further, encourages me,
yet to delve.

And so I take my cue, once again, and
affirm: I'm here now. I might as well make
the most of it. Whatever that turns out
to be: it probably really doesn't matter at
all, but for my soul—if nothing else—it's
better to sense me alive than just there;
more joyful than to reject, to embrace;
more gracious to receive what is given
with thanks; and wiser to do what I can,
but leave for someone else or another time
what I can't; more courageous to take the
challenge, than to say no; more human,